Aa

If I were an apple
And grew on a tree,
I think I'd fall down
On a good boy like me.
I wouldn't stay there
Giving nobody joy;
I'd fall down at once
And say, 'Eat me, my boy.'

Here are some apples on a tree. Is there one for each boy?
Draw a line from each apple to a boy to find out.

Bb

Baa, baa, black sheep,
Have you any wool?
Yes, sir. Yes, sir,
Three bags full.
One for the master and one
for the dame.
And one for the little boy
who lives down the lane.

Draw a bag of wool for each person in the rhyme.

Cc

Cobbler, Cobbler, mend my shoe,
Get it done by half past two;
Stitch it up, and stitch it down,
Then I'll give you half a crown.

The cobbler has mixed up all the shoes.
Which shoes go together?

Dd

Ding, dong, bell,
Pussy's in the well.
Who put her in?
Little Johnny Flynn.
Who pulled her out?
Little Tommy Stout.

There are *six* main differences between these two pictures. Can you spot them?

Ee

Engine, engine, number nine,
Sliding down Chicago line;
When she's polished she will shine,
Engine, engine, number nine.

Here is engine number nine. Colour her in bright colours.

Ff

One, two, three, four, five,
Once I caught a fish alive.
Six, seven, eight, nine, ten,
Then I let it go again.
Why did you let it go?
Because it bit my finger so.
Which finger did it bite?
This little finger on my right.

Untangle the fishing lines to find out who caught the fish.

Gg

Ten green bottles,
Standing on the wall.
Ten green bottles,
Standing on the wall.
And if one green bottle
Should accidentally fall –
There'll be nine green bottles
Standing on the wall.

Colour the bottles green. Count how many there are.

Hh

Humpty Dumpty sat on a wall.
Humpty Dumpty had a great fall.
And all the King's horses
And all the King's men,
Couldn't put Humpty
together again.

Draw Humpty Dumpty sitting on the wall. Give him a smiling face.

Incy Wincy spider
Climbing up the spout;
Down came the rain
And washed the spider out.
Out came the sunshine
And dried up all the rain;
Incy Wincy spider
Climbing up again.

Ii

Draw lots of raindrops coming down.
Draw a big sun to dry up the rain.

Jj

Jack and Jill
Went up the hill,
To fetch a pail of water;
Jack fell down
And broke his crown,
And Jill came tumbling after.

Here is Jack.

Find another one the same.

Here is Jill.

Find another one the same.

Kk

Old King Cole
Was a merry old soul,
And a merry old soul was he;
He called for his pipe,
And he called for his bowl,
And he called for his fiddlers three.

Here is a picture of a king for you to colour.

Ll

Lucy Locket lost her pocket,
Kitty Fisher found it;
Not a penny was there in it,
Only ribbon round it.

Which pocket belongs to Lucy Locket?

Mm

Mary, Mary, quite contrary,
How does your garden grow?
With silver bells and cockle shells,
And pretty maids all in a row.

Count the things in Mary's garden.

How many bells? ☐

How many shells? ☐

How many pretty maids? ☐

Nn

I had a little nut tree,
Nothing would it bear
But a silver nutmeg
And a golden pear.

Draw the silver nutmeg and the golden pear on the tree.

Oo

Oranges and lemons,
Say the bells of St Clements.
You owe me five farthings,
Say the bells of St Martins.
When will you pay me,
Say the bells of Old Bailey.
I do not know,
Says the great bell of Bow.

Colour the oranges orange and the lemons yellow.

Pp

Pat-a-cake, pat-a-cake,
baker's man,
Bake me a cake
as fast as you can;
Pat it and prick it
and mark it with B,
Put it in the oven
for baby and me.

How old are you? Draw the right number of candles on the cake.
Write your name on the cake.

Qq

The Queen of Hearts
She made some tarts,
All on a summer's day;
The Knave of Hearts
He stole those tarts,
And took them clean away.

The Knave of Hearts has hidden the tarts.
Find eight tarts and then colour the picture.

Rr

Round and round the garden
Like a teddy bear;
One step, two step,
Tickle you under there.

Teddy is lost in the garden. Draw a line to show his way out.

Ss

Sing a song of sixpence,
A pocket full of rye;
Four and twenty blackbirds,
Baked in a pie.
When the pie was opened,
The birds began to sing;
Wasn't that a dainty dish,
To set before a king?

Colour six singing blackbirds.

Tt

Twinkle, twinkle, little star,
How I wonder what you are.
Up above the world so high,
Like a diamond in the sky.

Draw some more stars twinkling in the sky.

Uu

I have a big umbrella,
Which hides me from the rain.
But when the sun comes out
once more,
I put it down again.

Colour the umbrella.

Use these colours: r –  g –  b – 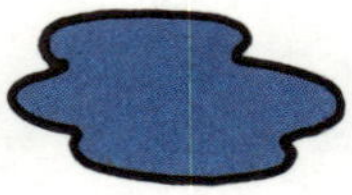

Vv

Roses are red,
Violets are blue,
Sugar is sweet,
And so are you!

Colour the violets blue.

How many roses? ☐

How many violets? ☐

Ww

Wee Willie Winkie
runs through the town,
Upstairs and downstairs
in his nightgown.
Rapping at the window,
crying through the lock,
Are the children all in bed,
it's past eight o'clock?

Which way does Wee Willie Winkie have to go
to see if the children are in bed?

Xx

Hot cross buns! Hot cross buns!
One a penny, two a penny,
Hot cross buns!

Draw a big X on each bun.

(Note: The actual sound of X is X as in box)

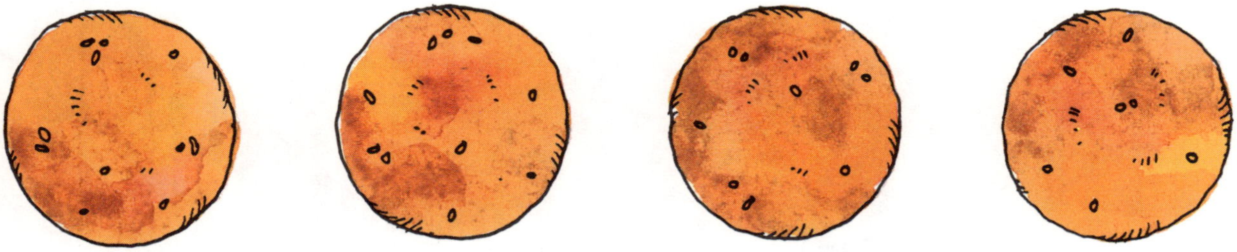

Yy

Yankee Doodle came to town,
Riding on a pony;
He stuck a feather in his hat
And called it macaroni.

Yankee Doodle had lots of hats.

Find another like this

like this

and like this

Zz

Of all the animals in the zoo,
I like the zebra best.
He's black and white
From nose to tail,
Just like my stripey vest.

Draw black stripes on this zebra.